she's sweet as...

international bestselling author
seven rue

Editing by Jennifer Marie
Cover design & formatting by Seven Rue

Find More Seven Rue

Website: www.authorsevenrue.com
Amazon: Seven_Rue
Instagram: @sevenrue
TikTok: @authorsevenrue
Reader Group on Facebook: Seven Rue's Taboos

Chapter 1

SINCLAIR

I met Archer in a bar five weeks ago, and back then, I never would've imagined I'd be as obsessed with him as I was now.

I've never wanted to be in a relationship, and in the beginning, I didn't think Archer wanted that either. But the more time we spent together, the more we slipped into the direction of becoming an actual couple.

I was a bit hesitant, but I was letting it happen.

I've always been very open, letting things come to me the way they were, and I never pushed or chased.

I attracted things. People. Men.

Especially men.

Older ones, just like Archer.

He had been watching me across the bar that night, his gaze burning through me for two full hours before I finally stared back.

The fire in our eyes ignited instantly, and it was clear that I'd go home with him that night.

And even when I let things happen naturally, I did let him work for more of my attention.

He had raised a brow at me, expecting me to walk over to him. But I stayed in my seat, giving him the same look back, silently telling him to make the first move.

He was stubborn, and so was I.

While he kept his deep blue eyes on me, I studied the rest of his handsome face to try and figure out how old he was.

His black hair didn't give me any hints of his age, but his whitening beard did. His hair was long enough to be tucked behind his ears back then, and it was perfectly styled—until he cut it short. He looked just as handsome with a buzzcut.

His beard wasn't too long, and I couldn't help but imagine how it would feel against my skin when I'd kiss him.

Or how it would feel brushing against my inner thighs, tickling my pussy.

I guessed him being in his late forties because he still looked young, and as it turned out later that night, I wasn't off by much.

Archer was fifty-three, exactly thirty years older than me, and that age gap turned me on a whole damn lot.

After another while of staring at each other, he finally gave in and got up from his seat, and as he walked over to me, I let my eyes wander all over his body.

He was tall, at least six-seven, his shoulders were broad, and his chest hard. Another strange thought appeared in my mind when I took in his large upper body.

Curled up, I was probably the same size. I was five-two.

He had no issue picking me up and holding me with one arm wrapped around my waist.

His lower body was not a disappointment either.

The pants he was wearing were tight enough to show off that big bulge right under his belt.

I could see his length pressing against the fabric. His cock was tucked to the side, and the outline of his tip could be seen near his right inner thigh.

Yet another sexual thought came to me. This time, I was in the air, his cock deep inside of me while I dangled from my arms he was holding behind my back.

It was a position I had seen in videos. One of those monster porn videos where a large creature with a huge cock fucked a human.

Not sure why those videos turned me on, but I knew I wasn't the only woman who liked them.

Archer was human, but he reminded me of one of those creatures. He was almost as large, and I loved the idea of his huge cock buried inside of me.

As he stood in front of me, his eyes moved all over my face and body, and once he decided to be pleased with what was in front of him, he finally spoke, instantly making my panties wet with his deep, dirty words.

"Instead of just thinking about my dick deep inside of you, why don't we make it happen?"

I couldn't deny my attraction.

I was done for in that very moment, and ten minutes later, I was kneeling in front of him in a dark alleyway.

Now, that wasn't really my style. I was classier than that. But Archer had promised to take me home right after sucking him off, and we both couldn't help ourselves.

So the alleyway had to do.

It's been five weeks of intense, hot sex and many sleepless nights, and tonight was the first time Archer would let me meet his friends.

He didn't tell me much about them but I knew that they were all single men in their fifties.

Some were divorced, some were forever bachelors.

I was excited to get to know the people Archer hung out with when he wasn't with me, and I was most excited to find out if he was as grumpy and dark as he was with me.

Archer parked his SUV in the bar's parking lot, and I looked toward the entrance where a guy with sunglasses and a buzzcut was guarding the door.

"How exclusive is this bar?" I asked, moving my gaze to Archer.

Today he chose to wear black pants and a black button-down shirt, leaving the top three buttons open to show off some of that sculpted chest.

He was checking his phone, and after pushing it back into his pocket, he turned to face me. "Exclusive enough to have someone guard the door."

I rolled my eyes at him.

Always so humorous.

I disregarded his non-informative reply and decided to check myself in the rearview mirror instead. I reached for it with my left hand and tilted it down and to the side until I saw myself in it.

Lifting my right hand to my lips, I brushed my thumb along the edge of my bottom lip to clean up my lipstick. "Are you gonna be this annoyed with me the whole night or will you turn into someone I don't recognize once we're with your friends?"

A deep chuckle left him. "You think I'll be treating you differently with my friends around?"

"Every man does. Wouldn't be surprised."

He was silent, watching me from the side while I continued to check my face for any flaws.

When the silence went on for too long, I moved my gaze to his to lock eyes with him. "I take your silence as a yes."

He clicked his tongue and dismissed me with a wave of his big hand. I loved his fingers around my throat, and I loved them inside of me. Archer never ceased to amaze me with how incredibly talented he was with his hands.

"You don't know what you're talking about, kid."

"Don't." I glared at him with annoyance. "You know I hate when you call me kid."

"Then stop saying shit like that. You're confident enough to suck my dick in public so be confident in what we have. I'm not gonna treat you any fucking different." His voice was raspy and low, and no matter what he said it turned me on.

It didn't help when I was mad. Every time that was the case, we ended up having angry sex wherever we happened to be.

Last time we were at a restaurant, and the men's restroom was the place we ended up spending the most time in.

Until we got kicked out for disturbance.

Instead of continuing the conversation we were having, I decided to end it with one simple statement. "I'm excited to meet your friends," I told him with a sweet smile.

He didn't respond with words. He did it with his body. My favorite way of his to reply to me.

He turned in his seat and reached out his hand to wrap his fingers around my throat, pulling me closer before he covered my mouth with his.

He kissed me roughly, his beard scratching my skin, and his lips messing up my lipstick.

I'd have to reapply after this, but for now, I let him mess up my makeup as much as he liked.

Chapter 2

SINCLAIR

He held on to my throat with a tight grip, and he tilted my head back so his tongue could dip deeper into my mouth.

He kept pushing it further down, almost reaching the back of my throat. His tongue felt fucking amazing.

Whenever he went down on me, he liked to fuck my asshole and pussy with it, and I loved feeling it slide in and out of me.

Archer loved to play with my ass. He loved licking it, fingering it, and he especially loved to fuck it.

We didn't shy away from anything—especially bodily fluids. But I was surprised the first time he emptied himself while being buried inside of me, filling my asshole with his hot piss.

It was a new experience, but the more he did it, the more I enjoyed it.

I wondered if Archer's friends knew about his fetishes.

His fingers tightened on my throat, and I had to hold my breath when no more air traveled through my airway.

His tongue curled around mine, then he sucked on it before pushing his deeper again, almost touching that dangly thing at the back of my throat.

A moan came out of me, and I reached out my hand to grip his shirt. We wouldn't get out of this car for a while, and things would get steamier in just minutes.

When he broke the kiss after sliding his tongue over mine one last time, he muttered under his breath, telling me to move over to him.

"Come sit on my lap, kitten."

Before I moved, he unbuckled his belt and unzipped his pants. I watched him pull down his pants and boxers, then he wrapped his hand around his thickness, rubbing the base and then squeezing his tip where a drop of precum was sitting.

I licked my lips, knowing just how good his cum tasted. It was addicting, and I loved having it on my tongue. I also loved when he came on my tits and stomach, rubbing his cum all over my body, and letting it dry into my skin.

"You gonna let me do all the work?"

I met his gaze for just a second before I shook my head. "Of course not, daddy."

I climbed over the center console to straddle his lap, and he helped me settle by placing both his hands on my waist.

His hands were almost big enough to reach around my body, his fingertips barely touching.

"That's a good girl. It was a good choice after all not to wear panties beneath this tiny skirt. I can push my cock right into that wet, tight pussy."

I gripped his shoulders with both hands and looked down at his cock pressing into my belly. His tip almost touched the undersides of my tits, and his length always reminded me how deep he could bury himself into me.

He filled me out perfectly, stretching me in a way I couldn't quite explain. I believed having his shaft pushed so deep inside of me couldn't be healthy for me. It surely wasn't right to have something so big inside of your pussy, but my body never gave me any alarming signals. I had gotten used to his size.

As he lifted my skirt to expose my bare pussy, I took a quick look to either side of me, checking for people in the parking lot.

No one was out there, but even if, it wouldn't have bothered us.

We were no strangers to being watched in public, and we wouldn't stop at much. We weren't ashamed. But of course, we did make sure not to be inappropriate in places where people who weren't supposed to see sexual things were around.

He pushed his hands under my skirt, holding my hips tightly as he lifted me enough to position himself at my entrance, and as if I was some type of sex doll, he pushed me down, making me slide down his cock with so much ease.

"OH!" I cried out and threw my head back, loving that burning sensation as his cock pushed into me.

"Goddamn," he groaned, his fingertips digging into my skin. "Let me see those tits, kitten. I wanna suck them."

I looked at him once I got used to him being inside of me, and while he held me there, I pulled up my top to expose my tits. I wasn't wearing a bra either, but then I never was.

I was lucky to have tits that held themselves up without help from a bra. I had other issues though. My blonde hair, for example, liked to get all curly and frizzy whenever there was even the slightest bit of humidity in the air, and it didn't help that we lived in Florida.

The left side of my face also liked to flare up at times, with dark red spots appearing, leaving me all itchy.

No doctor I had ever been to knew why my skin did that, so I learned to live with it.

It was annoying, and the flare-ups often happened at the most random moments. I luckily sensed them coming way before they actually happened though, and tonight, I had a good feeling that I wouldn't end up with red spots all over one side of my face.

"Come closer," he ordered, and I leaned in until he was close enough to pull one of my nipples into his mouth.

I started moving my hips, rocking back and forth, and feeling his cock twitch inside of me.

"Oh, yes!" I moaned as he pulled at my nipple with his teeth.

I moved my hands from his shoulders up to his hair, feeling the spikiness of his buzzcut.

He huffed after letting my nipple pop out of his mouth, and when he leaned back in his seat, he gripped my hips harder again to lift and lower me on top of him.

His length slid in and out of me slowly at first, but his thrusts quickened after he had adjusted himself.

It was easy for him to hold back on a climax, but even Archer had issues sometimes. Only when I teased him long enough, though.

"Dirty girl. Keep those pretty eyes on me, kitten. I wanna watch all those emotions flash through them. Fuck, baby, you're so goddamn beautiful."

My chest warmed as he drawled his words while using me like a damn pump, fucking me like I was made of plastic.

I loved how strong he was. How easily he lifted me, and how much control he had over me—even with just one hand touching me.

"You feeling me inside you, kitten?" he asked, his voice so damn sexy. "Feel my tip hitting the very back of your pussy?"

I nodded, wincing as he slammed me down harder.

"Wish I could fuck your mouth like this. I'm gonna make you choke on my dick later. Make you fucking gag. Shit, love, I wanna make you gag so fucking hard that you throw up."

Another fetish of his.

Not the throw-up itself, but the idea of me gagging and having to puke.

Just the thought of it made me want to throw up the first time he talked about it, but knowing how much it turned him on, I had let him do just that once before.

I did in fact gag, but I hadn't eaten enough that day to actually throw up.

Tonight, if I were to eat enough, he might just fulfill his need of seeing me miserable.

And him making me feel miserable by doing something so dirty did turn me on.

Guess I really was the right woman for him.

I definitely wasn't the only one who'd let him do all those nasty things to. I was just lucky enough to have caught his interest.

"Squeeze that pussy around my dick, baby. Make me fill you with my cum."

My moans got louder and my breathing heavier, and though I didn't have to, I started moving up and down, almost jumping on top of him while his cock stretched me wider.

I felt the veins along his shaft every time his cock pulsated.

His fingers dug deeper into my hips, and I took it as a warning. He didn't want me to move. He wanted to be in control, so I gave in and let him do what he did best.

He held me in place while he started thrusting his hips upward, fucking me hard. The sound of our thighs clashing was loud enough to be heard outside of the car, but I was pretty sure my moans and his groans were much louder.

"Oh God! Please—"

"Beg, kitten. Beg and I will fuck you so damn hard you'll pass out."

"PLEASE!" I cried. I was still holding on to his shoulder with one hand, and I pushed the other into my hair to stop it from sticking to my chest. I was sweating, and so was he. We'd have to go freshen up before meeting his friends. "Fuck me harder, Archer."

"So fucking gorgeous," he grunted as his thrusts quickened. "Gonna fuck you unconscious. Come on, baby. Come on my dick."

I was close, but I wanted to ride this out for as long as possible, and I wanted him to come at the same time.

"Don't hold back. Come."

I shook my head and my body tensed.

"Fucking hell, Sin. Come for me!" he demanded, thrusting even harder.

I ignored his words and kept tightening every muscle inside of me, knowing if I held on a little longer, that climax would be incredible.

But Archer knew how to make me explode.

The determination in his face almost scared me, and I knew I had no chance of pushing this orgasm out for much longer.

He kept holding me down with one hand on my hip, and he lifted his other to cup both my tits at once. His hand was *that* big.

His thumb and pinky each pressed into my nipples while his palm squeezed my tits simultaneously.

"OH YES!" In an instant, my body and mind crashed, making me feel dizzy

"That's it. Beautiful," I heard him say, but his voice was distant.

I wasn't passing out the way I hoped I would, but my brain was at the verge of shutting down.

My body collapsed on top of his, and as I leaned into him, he continued to fuck me.

He needed to reach his own climax, and when he would, I'd experience yet another extremely intense sensation.

I loved when his cum filled my pussy, warming me from the inside.

He stopped moving after a couple hard thrusts and gripped my hips with both hands again, then he pushed me down, burying his cock into me as deep as possible before emptying himself inside of me.

"GAAAH!"

I felt his cum fill me as he wrapped his arms tightly around my waist, holding me in place.

I whimpered and felt his cock twitch, his tip tickling that spot deep inside of me.

We both needed a minute to calm down, but once we did, he wrapped his large hand around my neck, making me lean back to face him again. He covered my mouth with his, kissing me deeply with his tongue.

"Wish I could stay like this with you forever, Kitten."

Archer might've been the grumpiest and gloomy man on this planet, but sometimes, he spoke the most romantic words.

It was rare, which was why I made sure to remember those words forever.

Chapter 3

SINCLAIR

I had no clue what his friends looked like. Therefore I had no idea we had passed them on our way to the restroom as we entered the bar.

"Over here," Archer said, placing his hand on my lower back and guiding me toward one of the booths.

The bar war dimly lit, with burgundy booths and black tables.

There were men mostly in this bar—only two other women were around.

The smell of cigars and whiskey filled the room, but it didn't bother me much. I was focused on my man and the ones he was walking me over to.

"There he is," one of the four men sitting at the booth said, smirking up at Archer but never moving his eyes over to me. "What's taken so long?"

Archer didn't reply. He simply nudged me toward the bench on the other side of the table, making me sit down next to one of the men.

Archer came to sit next to me, his hand immediately touching my thigh. "Boys, this is my woman, Sinclair." He then looked at me, introducing me to his friends without pointing at each of them to make sure I knew who he was referring to. "That's Link, Renner, Ford, and Tabor."

I looked at the four of them, nodding to show them my acknowledgement, but I still didn't get even a look from them.

Great.

They clearly didn't want me here, but I wasn't going to let them make me uncomfortable.

Archer wanted me here, and that was all that mattered.

"What do you wanna drink?" he asked, leaning closer.

"Coke, please."

"No alcohol?"

"No, thanks." I smiled at him before placing a kiss to his jaw. I felt him tense, and he cleared his throat when he sat up straight again.

Was he ashamed of me?

No. He wouldn't have taken me here if that was the case.

I looked around the table again, taking in all the mens' cigars. They were all wearing a dark shirt, all top three buttons open, and showing off their chest hair.

They had to be around Archer's age if not slightly older.

Two of them had gray beards and their hair was whitening too, and while the few crinkles showed signs of aging, their bodies definitely didn't.

It looked like they all worked out, though, they were so huge that it didn't necessarily have to be muscle mass that made them so...large.

I hadn't seen them standing up yet, but I was pretty damn sure they were about the same height as Archer.

A waitress approached our table and Archer ordered our drinks, and one of the others asked for another whiskey.

I had a feeling that I wouldn't be talking much tonight, but I didn't mind. As long as I could spend time with Archer, everything was alright.

After getting our drinks, I reached for my glass and took a sip, using the moment to eye every single one of Archer's friends.

I couldn't read them. They all looked grumpy. One of them seemed angry, but mostly, they were all so damn serious.

I put my glass back down and adjusted my skirt, then I nudged closer to Archer to lean against his side and listened in on their conversation.

To be fair, I had no clue what the topic of conversation was, especially when all the sentences they spoke didn't include more than four words each.

Fun. This is so much fun.

I looked down at my lap and placed both my hands on Archer's. He was still gripping my thigh, and to remind him of my presence, I pushed his hand between my thighs and against my pussy.

He knew immediately what I was doing, and knowing Archer, he wouldn't stop me.

But what I didn't know was him being the one pushing it further.

He spread his fingers and pushed apart my thighs, making my skirt ride up enough to expose my pussy again.

I looked up at him, noticing that he was focused on the conversation he was having.

Still, without looking, he knew exactly what he was doing.

It was dark enough to hide what was happening underneath the table, but I had already noticed glances from two of Archer's friends.

They knew, but they didn't say a thing. They didn't care, and neither did I.

If this was the only way to have Archer's attention for the rest of the night, then I was okay with it.

I licked my lips and looked up at Archer again, widening my legs further to give him more space.

But when I spread my legs, I touched the knee of the guy sitting to my right.

I turned my head to look at him, but instead of meeting his eyes, I saw him staring down at Archer's hand.

For a moment I thought he was going to complain. Instead, he watched Archer's fingers tease my pussy for a little while before he lifted his gaze to continue conversing with the others.

Damn...nothing fazed these men.

A soft moan escaped me as Archer pushed two fingers inside of me, without warning. I was wet enough to have them slide right into me, but I wasn't as relaxed as I was back in the car earlier.

Still, I let him play with me.

"Heard anything from Manny?" The man next to me asked. His question was directed at Archer, and I looked up at him to await his response.

Who is Manny? Do I even wanna know?

"Haven't heard from him in weeks. Not that I want to. He's got nothing nice to say anyway."

His voice was dark and raspy as usual, and something about him saying those words so nonchalant made my pussy clench.

"Manny won't contact you anyway. Forget that shit," the one opposite of Archer said.

"The fuck do you know, Renner?" the man next to me replied.

Renner was the one with the neck tattoos, *I suppose.*

I finally had one name down. Three more to go and I knew everyone's names.

"If you really need to know, I saw him downtown two days ago. I briefly talked to him, and what he had to say was not something you wanna hear. Trust me."

All the men raised a brow at Renner, and they didn't look convinced at all.

Archer muttered under his breath, and so did the one next to me.

Gee, whatever business they had going on with Manny, I hoped they wouldn't continue talking about it.

I obviously wasn't allowed to know about it. The only thing Archer ever told me about his work was that he had many clients who were richer than I could ever imagine, and that they dealt with even richer people and businesses.

"We'll talk about this another time," Archer grunted.

"Why, you busy with something else right now?" the man next to me said, and when I turned to look at him, he was smirking.

"You're sitting right next to them," Renner stated, amused. "You should be able to answer your own damn question, Ford."

Ford.

Two names down, two more to go.

Ford looked at Archer's hand again, his fingers still deep inside of me.

I felt my face heat up, my cheeks blushing as I felt all eyes on me now.

Finally, they were giving me attention.

"Stop looking at my woman," Archer muttered, but even he was smirking, not taking this seriously at all. "Either that, or you join in. My kitten's a naughty one. She won't mind."

I didn't come here with big expectations. But what I never *ever* would've expected was Archer sharing me with his friends.

Chapter 4

SINCLAIR

Archer pulled his fingers out of me and reached for my hand, placing it on my pussy and directing two of my fingers inside.

"Let Ford taste how sweet you are, kitten," he said, then he lifted his arm and wrapped it around my shoulders.

While I fingered myself, Archer pulled me back against his chest, making me turn more toward Ford.

I looked at him, wondering if he'd rather taste me on my fingers or directly from my pussy.

He wasn't moving, so it was in my hands to decide.

I dropped my gaze to my hand and watched as I slid in and out of my wetness, and once my fingers were covered with my juices, I pulled them back out and held them in front of Ford's mouth.

His lips curled, and I watched as he reached for my wrist to pull my hand closer to him. My fingertips grazed his bottom lip, and when his mouth parted, he pulled my fingers inside to taste me.

He closed his eyes while he sucked on them, and I couldn't tear mine off him. He was enjoying it.

He curled his tongue around my fingers before letting them pop out of his mouth. He kept holding on to my wrist, and when his eyes finally met mine, he grinned widely. "Tastes like heaven."

"Thank you," I managed to say under my breath.

"Told you. My kitten's a sweet one." Archer reached all the down to my right leg, pushing it further out until I had to lift it over Ford's lap.

He placed both his hands on my leg, pulling it even closer until I was sitting almost horizontally on the bench.

Without asking for permission, Ford reached between my legs and started playing with my pussy. His fingertips grazed my folds, then he started rubbing my clit with his thumb, circling it slowly, teasing me.

Archer let his friend touch me, and as long as he didn't have issues with that, I wouldn't have any either.

I kept watching Ford as I couldn't look at Archer, but I smiled when he reached down my top and cupped one of my tits, squeezing it hard and pinching my nipple.

"I'll handle Manny," Archer then stated nonchalant, as if he wasn't touching me in that very moment.

The others went back to talking about business, but I didn't listen to what they were saying. For the first time, I was worrying about what others might think.

The bar wasn't packed, but there were enough people around to notice that something sexual was going on in one of the corners.

I looked up from Ford's hand and moved my gaze from one booth to the other, and then over to the bar.

Alarms started going off in my head when the waitress from before walked over to our table with that friendly smile of hers, and when she stopped, she let her eyes wander all over my body.

I swallowed the lump that had suddenly formed in my throat. I was waiting for her to say something. To tell me that I'd get kicked out of this bar. I was even expecting her to make rude remarks, telling me how slutty it was of me to let these men touch me in a public space.

But she didn't do any of those things.

To my surprise, she turned to the guys and asked them if she could bring us more to drink.

They ordered another round, then she was off again, not saying a word about what was playing out in front of her eyes.

I was confused and astonished at the same time.

I had expected at least a nasty glare from the waitress. Or an annoyed and disgusted sigh from anyone else in this bar.

But there was nothing.

No one cared, and when that realization hit, I relaxed.

"Tabor owns this place. What happens here, stays here," were Archer's dark words in my ear.

My chest rose and fell with his hand still cupping my tit, and when he used his forefinger to point at one of the guys, I followed it to see who Tabor was.

It was the man to Ford's right, the one with the icy blue eyes, which meant that the man next to Archer was called Link. The one with the darker skin.

So this was normal.

All these people had probably seen or even done worse than what was going on at our booth, and while it was strange thinking about it, it turned me on.

The waitress returned, setting their drinks onto the table. And as if Ford noticed my discomfort with her appearing just earlier, he started fingering me harder, making me moan out loud with the waitress standing there, watching.

"Dirty girl. Can't get enough," Ford murmured as I lifted my hips to meet his thrusts, and I moved my gaze to him again, watching him admiring me.

He thought I was beautiful. He didn't have to say it out loud, and it only made me more confident.

SIN

"I wanna hear her moan again. That sweet sound that came out of her just now was a nice little tease. I wanna hear more." Tabor was the one who spoke, and I moved my gaze to his, finding that same admiration in his eyes.

He kept looking, and Ford did just what his friend wanted.

His fingers curled inside of me, rubbing against my walls as he continued to finger me. His movements were fast, and he pushed deeper after every time he pulled back.

He kept using his thumb to rub my clit, and I moved my hips in circles to get him to touch me exactly where I wanted him to.

"Oh!" I cried, leaning more into Archer as he tightened his arm around me.

His hand squeezed my tit again before moving on to the other, pinching my nipple with his forefinger and thumb.

"You like that, don't you, kitten? Having someone else touch you while I'm right here watching."

"She likes to be shared," Link added, and while he hadn't talked much, I agreed with him.

I did like being shared but I hoped nothing would change after tonight between Archer and me.

I really liked him, and as long as he was okay with this, I was too.

"I will share her with you now, but she'll be mine alone after tonight," Archer said, and after a long pause, he added, "Unless she wants to do this all over again one day."

So he was giving me a choice while still being possessive. I liked that. Hell, it made me like him even more.

I smiled and moaned again as Ford's fingers dug deeper into me. "Sure would be a shame to never see her again after this," Tabor drawled before taking a sip of his whiskey. "She's sweet as sin."

"She's gotta be." Archer cupped both my tits with his large hand like he had done in the car earlier, then he leaned in again, his mouth at my ear as he murmured, "It's in her name."

I reached my first climax of the night in that very moment, and nothing could've ever prepared me for what was to come next.

CHAPTER 5

ARCHER

I didn't bring women here. Never had, and I thought I never would.

But things with Sinclair turned out different than I had imagined.

I saw her as a quick fuck. A one-night-stand. Someone I would forget the morning after, but that never happened.

Instead, I found myself lusting over her. Being a possessive ass and needing to know where she was all the fucking time.

I acted like a damn highschooler. Like a teenage boy who had a crush on the head-cheerleader, hoping to get her attention.

I had her attention alright.

And now I had her showing off those sweet tits and that wet pussy to my friends.

It didn't bother me. Not tonight.

I continued to play with those sweet tits of hers while my oldest friend, Ford, fingered her pussy.

She was enjoying the attention my friends gave her, and I had noticed that when that hadn't been the case when we got here, she was upset about it.

She looked unsure and wondered why my friends didn't look at her. But I knew the reason.

They were being respectful toward me. They waited for me to give them the okay to go for it. To show my woman some affection.

Tonight, they could do just that.

And depending on the outcome, they might get another night with her.

I leaned in and rested my chin on her shoulder, nibbling at her ear before whispering, "How about that blowjob we talked about in the car?"

She turned her head enough so that I could see her eyes, and the excitement flashing in them made me smirk.

Dirty girl.

She loved to wrap her lips around my cock, and I especially loved how tiny her mouth was compared to my shaft.

I knew she had a fetish for large men, and luckily, I was one. It wasn't always an advantage to be this big though—having pain in both knees and my hips was something I could easily live without—but when women like Sinclair enjoyed my size, I pushed the pain aside.

I knew I wasn't the only one here struggling with aches and stings in certain places, but that's what we had to deal with while aging.

We weren't the youngest anymore. Though, I knew Sinclair would never switch us out for some guys her age.

I watched as she licked her lips before biting her bottom one, and when she nodded, I was pulled right out of my thoughts, reminding myself of what I had just offered her.

She moved, gently pushing Ford's hand off her, then she turned in my arms until she was kneeling on the bench between me and Ford.

I brushed her hair aside, needing to see that beautiful face of hers.

It didn't matter if she was wearing makeup or not, or if her face flared up like it sometimes did. Sinclair was always beautiful, and I often sat there staring at her, admiring her.

And this will freak her out if she'd ever find out, but I liked to watch her when she was asleep too.

She was just so goddamn gorgeous.

"We can't see from here," Tabor stated from across the table.

I pulled Sinclair's hair into a ponytail at the back of her head, then I looked over at him, raising a brow.

"Then find a better spot. I'm not moving. And neither is she."

I tightened my grip on Sin's hair, moving my gaze to her hands which were now unbuckling my belt.

She didn't hesitate. "Needy slut," I hissed, watching closely as her fingers worked on the button of my pants.

She opened it, then unzipped the zipper before pulling at the waistband of my pants.

I lifted off the bench to help her, and once my pants and boxer briefs were far enough down, she reached for my shaft and pulled it out.

I knew my cock felt heavy in her hand. That tiny hand that was barely able to wrap fully around my thickness.

She steadied my length with both her hands at my base, and after a couple of seconds of admiring my cock, she finally dipped down her head to pull my tip into her mouth.

Tabor and Renner moved, wanting to see exactly what was happening, and once they were in a good position, they smirked as if it was their cocks being sucked.

"Shit, she's so damn tiny, it doesn't fully fit in her mouth," Renner said.

"I'll make it fit," I growled.

I gave her a moment to adjust, but when my cock throbbed for the fifth time, I took over.

I pushed her head down until my tip hit the back of her throat, and when she gagged, I heard my friends around me groan.

I didn't have to look up to see their need to have their dicks sucked in their eyes, and I also didn't have to look up to see what they were doing with their hands.

They were rubbing their cocks above their pants, watching as my kitten chocked on mine.

"That's it, baby. Keep that mouth open so I can fuck it," I ordered.

I held her still with both my hands cupping her head, then I started thrusting my hips upward, fucking her mouth hard.

I saw Ford take off his jacket out of the corner of my eye, then he moved, turning more toward Sinclair.

"Let me get another taste of that pussy," I heard him say, and shortly after, Sinclair squealed.

I had no doubt she'd want to do this all over again once we were done, but she had no idea how tired and exhausted she was going to be.

Chapter 6

SINCLAIR

There was so much going on around me but I couldn't focus on anything other than Archer's cock in my mouth, and Ford's tongue sliding through my folds.

The other three were watching, and the simple thought of that turned me on.

Archer's hands were big enough to cover the back and sides of my head and feeling Ford's hands on my ass as he flicked his tongue against my clit, I knew his were just as big.

All these men were over six feet, almost seven feet tall, and I couldn't stop imagining them playing around with my body as if I were a doll.

A choking sound came out of me when Ford's fingers grazed my asshole, and after he wet it with his tongue, he pushed two fingers inside of me.

They weren't as thick as Archer's. Then again, Archer liked to push more than just two fingers into my ass.

He liked to fuck me there with his cock too.

One time, he had fisted me. But not in the ass. I wouldn't have survived that.

I almost chuckled at my thoughts, but I couldn't. The only noises I could make were gagging sounds and moans.

"Look at her. So damn submissive," one of the men said. Renner, maybe? No. His voice was way deeper.

I arched my back a little more as Ford pushed his fingers deeper into my ass, and Archer thrusted his hips harder, burying himself deep into my mouth.

I felt his tip at the back of my throat, and if I relaxed a little more, he would push it down even further.

We all know what happened the last time he did that.

I wasn't keen on throwing up in the middle of a bar. Then again, I had no control over this.

Archer pulled back my head and grunted loudly once his cock popped out of my mouth.

"I gotta fuck that mouth right," he said, making me wonder what position he would put me in next.

He got up from the bench and left me kneeling there with Ford still playing with my pussy and asshole.

I looked up to watch Archer get rid of his pants and boxer briefs, and once he stood there in his t-shirt, he needed a moment to take in the scene going on behind me.

There was a gleam of possession in his eyes, jealousy taking over quickly after realizing that he wasn't the only one touching and pleasing me.

He'd have to live with that though.

He let his friends join, and he'd be the asshole if he'd tell them to stop now.

Though, I was pretty damn sure that when Archer told them to leave, they would.

"I want her on the table," Archer demanded, and Ford was gone from behind me in an instant.

I pushed myself up to sit back on my feet, and as I wiped away the saliva from the corners of my mouth, I looked at the five men surrounding me.

This was a dream.

Of course, having Archer there was important to me, but I couldn't help but smile at the fact that four more men were going to play with me. Share me.

They wanted me, and I would give myself to them.

"Come here, kitten," Archer demanded, and I crawled to the end of the bench before standing up.

He reached for my hand and pulled me to him, pressing my body against his. With his hands moving to my hips, he gripped the waistband of my skirt and pushed it down. "We want you naked and on the table. On your back."

I looked up at him with wide eyes, admiring how handsome he looked when the crease between his brows was deep.

I also decided in that very moment that I liked him better with a buzzcut than long hair.

I gave him a nod, then let him take off my top before he turned me around. He gripped my hips and lifted me as if I was a bag of feathers, and he placed me onto the round table.

The others had already moved our glasses to make sure I wouldn't knock them over.

The table was cold and not comfortable to lie on, but I wouldn't care about all that once we continued to openly have fun in Tabor's bar.

I could sense the other people's eyes on me at times, but that didn't bother me either. I liked to be watched, and I liked to be the center of attention.

Naked or not.

Archer's hands were on my head once more, and he pulled me back until my shoulders were on the edge of the table.

"Lay your head back," he ordered.

I looked up and saw his bare upper body. He had taken off his shirt, and around me, the others were undressing as well.

"Now, I want you to open your mouth and keep it open. I'll fuck this mouth so damn good, kitten, that jaw of yours will get stuck."

Even if that sounded bad, I hoped to end up with some pain.

"And I'm gonna fuck this mouth so deeply, you'll feel my cock all the way down your throat. Gonna have to hold your breath, baby."

He was warning me, trying to scare me, but nothing he'd ever say would make me stop him.

His words would only make me want more, and I couldn't wait to show him and the others how much I was able to take.

Chapter 7

ARCHER

I made sure Sinclair was comfortable enough on the table, and once I was sure of that, I grabbed her neck with both my hands and pushed her head further back, making it hang over the table's edge.

"Open," I demanded, and she parted her lips wide.

My tip was touching her cheek, and I moved my hips so that it was right at her mouth. "Keep it open. Tongue out."

She did as I said, then I pushed my cock into her mouth, sliding along her tongue until I saw my tip nudge against the inside of her throat. "Fuuuck," I groaned, keeping myself there for a moment until she gagged, then I pulled back and let her take a breath. "Focus, kitten. Don't want you to turn blue."

She gave me a small nod, and I gently brushed my thumbs along her neck while slowly filling her mouth again.

While I did, I looked at the guys surrounding the table, and I watched as Tabor stepped closer to it on the other side of me.

He placed both his hands on Sin's ankles, then he moved them up over her lower legs, stopping at her knees before moving his hands back down to her feet.

He admired her body, taking in every inch while the others started touching her all over.

Their hands were on her thighs, her belly, her tits, and I knew their touch was soaking her pussy.

Her body was relaxed and she was enjoying every second of this.

My naughty kitten.

A smirk tugged at my lips. I would take her here more often, that was for sure.

"Do I need to use a condom or can I fuck her bare? Sure would be a shame to put something between us," Tabor said, his voice low and dry.

I looked down to watch my cock disappear in her mouth once more. I never used a condom with her, other than that time I fucked her ass for the first time. I needed that condom to make it easier to fuck that tight hole, and I also needed a whole lot of lube.

Sinclair was tiny, but she's gotten used to my size by now.

I looked up again, thinking for a short moment before allowing my friend to go bare. "You don't need to use one. I trust you all to be clean."

Tabor nodded, and while the other three kept touching my girl, he unbuckled his belt to get rid of his pants and boxer briefs.

Once they were off, I didn't look at them anymore.

I had to focus on myself before I climaxed sooner than I wanted to and embarrassed myself in front of my oldest friends.

"That's it, kitten. Keep that mouth wide open." My tip pushed against her throat again, making a bump appear at the front of her neck. I grazed it with my thumb. "Fuuuck," I groaned slowly, teasing myself through her skin.

She gagged again, but instead of pulling back, I stayed buried inside of her for a while longer. "Focus," I reminded her, and her body relaxed again. "Good girl. You gonna have to take more than my cock tonight. I need that sweet body of yours to be all relaxed and ready."

"You sure she's able to take us all?" Renner asked, his hand squeezing Sinclair's left tit.

I didn't look up at him to make sure I stayed focused on her mouth around my cock. "She can take it. But the second she tells us to stop, we will. Understand?"

The guys grumbled in agreement. I didn't want any of them to hurt my kitten. If they did, the night would be over quickly.

SINCLAIR

I loved being touched by all these hands, feeling the roughness and different textures of their fingers on my skin.

All of them were being gentle at first, but the more I got used to them touching me, the more they allowed themselves to be rougher.

I didn't mind. As long as Archer was right there.

I had tears in my eyes from not being able to breathe normally, but I wasn't struggling. Archer was thrusting his hips slowly, pushing deeper into my mouth every time.

I loved how thick his cock was, and how much those veins stuck out and pressed against my tongue. And my pussy clenched on command every time his shaft throbbed,.

Tabor was the one teasing my inner thighs with his hands. He hadn't touched my pussy yet, but I knew the moment he would, my body would react intensely.

The sounds coming out of me were muffled. I wished I could make a noise, show the five of them just how good they made me feel. But I was certain that they already knew.

They were enjoying this. Me being so submissive and having them do whatever they wanted to me.

My walls clenched when I felt Tabor's fingertips graze my folds, and I arched my back when another pair of hands pulled apart my legs even further.

"I need to watch you fuck her. Shit, that pussy is soaking wet," I heard Link mutter. "Sure we'll fit?"

Tabor laughed harshly. "Doesn't matter if we fit. We'll make it fit."

"Think she can take two of us at the same time?" I heard Renner ask in that usual annoyed tone of his. Was he even glad to be here? Maybe his annoyance wasn't a reaction he had on me, but rather on his friend who was going to fuck me first.

"You're not gonna fuck her pussy and ass without me being in at least one of those tight holes," Archer said, his words clear and stern. "And I'm telling you this one last time and I hope you listen carefully. If she's hurting, we're stopping."

They didn't have to hear him say it again, but they once more agreed to not piss him off.

Chapter 8

SINCLAIR

Archer had pulled his cock out of my mouth and lifted my head, telling me to look at Tabor.

He was rubbing his hardness, spitting on it before he rubbed it in, then he positioned his tip at my entrance.

I wasn't sure why Archer wanted me to watch. I was perfectly fine being face-fucked by him without seeing what the others were doing.

But I wasn't going to fight it.

Tabor's eyes were fixated on my pussy, and while his left hand was holding on to my thigh, he was stroking his base intensely.

He wasn't pushing too hard at first, but once his tip slid inside of me, he thrusted his hips forward until his shaft disappeared.

I cried out as a sharp pain rushed through my body. I was used to that pain, and I knew it would be gone in a couple of seconds.

I took a deep breath while he stretched me from the inside, and when I moved my gaze to look at him, his eyes met mine.

"Fuck, darling. Nothing's ever been this damn tight." His eyes wandered down my body, then back up to meet mine again. "You want my cum inside of you?"

I nodded, biting my bottom lip. "Yes, please."

"Beg for it then." A smug grin pulled at his lips, and the arrogance in his eyes only made me want more.

These men knew the power they held, and especially Tabor being the owner of this bar, it was clear to him that anything he wanted, he'd get.

There was no reason for me to tell him no.

"Fuck me," I whispered, watching Tabor's face closely.

"I said to beg, not order me to fuck you."

"Please!" I cried out when his cock twitched inside of me. "Please, fuck me hard."

"That's it." He grunted and started thrusting into me.

Ford and Renner stepped closer to his side, and both of them grabbed one of my legs to keep them apart.

Ford caressed my right leg from my ankle to my thigh, and Renner rested my left against his body, with my foot barely reaching his chest.

I was surrounded by these insanely big men, and though the people around us knew what we were doing, I wasn't so sure they could actually see me on the table.

These men were covering me like a curtain, but the thought of people getting a glimpse of my naked body being used by these five men was the biggest turn on.

And while I would enjoy every single moment of this, I was excited to have Archer to myself again.

My feelings for him grew with every minute that passed, and I knew after this we would be certain that this thing between us was serious.

As if he heard my thoughts, he pressed his thumbs against my throat, cutting off my airway. "My naughty kitten," he said, his voice low. "Letting my friends fuck her. God, baby, I'm so fucking lucky you're mine."

I looked up at him, admiring him as he tightened his hands around my neck.

I couldn't speak, but I hoped my eyes told him everything I was feeling.

I was pleased when the slightest smile pulled at the corner of his mouth, then I moved my eyes back to the three men in front of me as he loosened his grip.

"Fuuuck," Tabor groaned as he moved faster. "Gonna fill this pussy with so much damn cum that it'll squirt out of you."

"Oh yes, please!" I begged.

I wanted to keep watching, but Archer had a different plan. He tilted my head back and without a warning, he pushed his cock back into my mouth.

I tasted his precum on my tongue, immediately wanting more.

I started to wonder how the other men tasted but I would soon find out.

My body started shaking when I felt someone's fingers on my clit. The way those fingers were positioned, it could've only been Ford touching me there.

The way he circled his fingertips on my clit made me cry out again, and I lifted my hips to meet Tabor's thrusts.

There were hands everywhere. Archer's were still on my head.

Each of my tits were then being cupped, and again, that only could've been Link.

His fingers pinched my nipples, and soon after, I heard him spit. It covered my tits, and he used his hands to rub it into my skin. "Goddamn. Look at those sweet tits glistening," Link murmured, letting me know that it was in fact him playing with my tits.

"Wait until you see this tight pussy. It's so damn soaked. I slide in and out of it so fucking easily," Tabor said, sounding amazed.

"I want to fuck that ass first," Renner added, and the second he spoke those words, Archer pulled his cock out of my mouth.

"No, I'll be the only one fucking her ass. Don't want her to get hurt."

He wasn't saying that because he thought his friends were bigger than him. He said that because he knew exactly how to fuck me without hurting me.

Also, I knew his possessiveness was another reason why he wouldn't let his friends go in the backdoor.

"Too damn bad," Renner muttered.

"Don't worry. Her pussy's just as tight," Tabor assured.

I was looking at him again, and I saw the veins in his neck stand out. He was close, and I prepared myself for him to come.

"GAAAH!" he groaned loudly, fucking me harder while Ford's fingers moved faster on my clit.

"Ohmygod," I breathed, circling my hips. I kept my eyes on Tabor's cock sliding in and out of me, and I felt my orgasm building deep inside of me, starting at my toes, and moving all the way up to my chest.

"Make her come," Archer ordered, giving me the rest of what was needed to make me climax.

I moaned loudly as my body jerked. They held me down, waiting for Tabor to finally unload inside of me.

"Holy fucking hell. That's it, darling. God, I marked this pussy now."

I liked every single thing they did and said to me, but Tabor's last words made me feel strange.

I tensed, and Archer had the same reaction. "That pussy is mine. No matter how many fucking times I let you come inside of her, she'll always be mine."

Chapter 9

ARCHER

No woman had ever made me feel this way. I was addicted to her. To her mind, her body. Her scent. Fuck, she was consuming me, and it didn't help how she was looking at me in that very moment.

Her eyes were wide, teary, and her lips parted. Her cheeks were flushed, and her neck was stained with red spots from my touch.

She had just come down from her high, and she wasn't taking her eyes off me.

I leaned down and kissed her lips, pulling her bottom lip between my teeth and nibbling on it before breaking the kiss. "You're mine," I whispered in a serious tone, and she nodded to agree with me. "I'm gonna give you a bit of time to calm down, but after that, I will fuck your ass so damn hard that you won't remember tonight."

"As good as that sounds, I hope I do remember," she whispered, her voice so damn sweet.

Smirking, I pressed another kiss to her lips before standing up straight again. "We'll see about that."

The guys stepped back but stayed close to the table, not putting away their cocks. They knew we'd continue soon enough, but they were giving Sinclair some space.

I brushed through her hair and watched Tabor pull out of her, and as he admired her cum-covered pussy, he grinned like a teenage boy who's had sex for the first time ever. "Look at that shit. Fucking beautiful."

My eyes narrowed, and an interesting thought crossed my mind. The guys and I had experimented with women before. We had done stuff none of us were ever prepared for, but I knew what I was going to tell him next was something he wouldn't turn down.

"Taste yourself on her."

Tabor looked up at me, and something flashed in his eyes. He looked down again as he ran his fingers through her slit with a smug grin on his face. "I might just do that."

Sinclair was resting the back of her head against my abs, and I kept caressing her face as we all watched Tabor kneel before her while Ford and Renner spread her legs wider.

Tabor's tongue came out to lick through her folds, and I could see his cum covering his tongue as when he pulled back slightly.

"Goddamn," Renner murmured, watching Tabor just as intensely as we were. "Must taste like heaven."

Tabor smirked, looking up at Tabor before his eyes met Sin's. "Even better."

Sinclair shivered and her hips jerked when he lowered his mouth to her pussy again. "Oh."

"You like that, baby?" I asked, brushing my thumb over her chin. Her gaze shifted, looking up at me with that intense gleam.

She nodded, smiling softly. "I do. But I miss your mouth."

I knew where she missed it, but it was Tabor's turn now. I leaned down and kissed her passionately, then I pushed my tongue between her lips and dipped it deep into her mouth, tasting myself on her tongue.

She moaned into the kiss, and when I pulled back, I looked into her eyes while wiping my spit off the side of her mouth. "You ready for more?"

She studied me for a moment, then finally nodded. "Yes."

I helped her sit up on the table, and once Tabor stepped away from her, the others did too. I pulled her to me, lifting her, and wrapping her legs around my waist.

Her wetness pressed against my skin, and I grunted when my tip grazed her ass.

Goddamn.

"I need to be inside you," I whispered against her forehead before pressing a kiss to it.

I sat down on the bench, further away from the table where we'd have more space.

Sinclair was straddling my lap, and she wrapped her arms around my neck, smiling at me with the most pleased look on her face.

I chuckled, studying her closely. "You're enjoying this a whole damn lot, aren't you?"

She nodded, her fingers gently running along my spine starting from my neck.

"You're still gonna tell me when it's getting too much, okay?"

"Okay."

I cupped her ass and squeezed it tightly, and I moved closer to take her mouth again. I kissed her hard, curling my tongue around hers.

She pressed her crotch against me, making my cock settle right between her folds.

As much as I was enjoying this, we didn't stay in that position for too long.

I broke the kiss and moved my hands to her waist. "Get up and turn around," I ordered.

She did as I said, and once she stood there in front of me, I let my eyes wander all over her backside, moving my hands along her sides.

"Beautiful," I heard Link say, and I agreed with a simple nod.

Beautiful and smart. Sexy and so damn sensual.

And she was all mine, even if I was sharing her with my oldest friends.

Chapter 10

SINCLAIR

Archer pulled me back to make me stand between his legs, and I steadied myself on his knees on either side of me as his hands gripped my hips tightly.

"Holly," I heard him say loudly, and the waitress from before walked over to us.

"Yes, sir?"

Sir. No, I don't like that.

"Please bring us olive oil."

"Yes, sir." She left without asking questions, but I had many.

Olive oil?

"Relax, baby. Can't fuck this tight ass without some kind of lube," Archer advised.

Oh. Oh!

I nodded as if I had already known what he wanted that oil for. When Holly was back, she handed him a small bottle of olive oil, and without looking at any of us, she left again.

I looked up at the four men standing in front of me. They were all rubbing their cocks, looking at my body and face.

"You like taking it up your ass, darling?" Tabor asked with a daring gleam in his eyes.

I looked up at him and nodded, unable to hide a proud smile that I was able to handle someone as big as Archer.

I whimpered when I felt Archer's wet fingers slide through my slit, circling my asshole before pushing two of them inside.

"This is gonna make it easier for me, kitten. Fuck, I'm gonna slide in and out of this ass so fucking fast."

I turned my head to look back at him, and I smiled when I saw the admiration in his eyes. "I can't wait," I whispered, arching my back a little more.

He put the oil aside, then I felt his tip at my entrance, gently pushing into me.

I relaxed, wanting to make this comfortable for the both of us.

I kept my hands on his knees, and when I felt Archer's on my hips again, I knew what was coming next.

"Deep breath," he demanded, and a second later, he pulled me back, sliding into me with his hardness.

I cried out as a sharp pain sliced through me. "Ow!" I wasn't in as much pain as I made it sound, it was just the first reaction my body had to Archer's cock filling me.

"Easy," he muttered. He reached around my body and gripped both my tits, pulling me back against his body. "That's it, kitten. You feeling okay?"

I nodded, unable to use my voice as I felt his cock throb inside of me.

"Link, you go first."

I looked up at Link and watched him grin as he stepped closer, still rubbing his shaft. "Lift your legs," he ordered, nodding toward Archer's knees.

He helped me position myself the way Link envisioned, and he held me with one arm wrapped around my waist. I rested my head on Archer's shoulder and observed Link as he moved between our legs.

He leaned in, placing his left hand on the wall behind us, and he lowered his hips until his tip touched my pussy.

His thickness scared me, but only because I would soon have the both of them inside of me.

"Calm. Easy," Archer whispered into my ear before licking my neck. "You can always tell us to stop if you need us to."

I nodded, but we both knew that wouldn't happen. I'd be in deep ecstasy the second they were both in me, and I wouldn't come out of it for a while.

Link's right hand was tightly wrapped around his base, and after sliding his tip through my slit for a while, he finally pushed into me.

"AAAH!"

"You feel that, baby?" Archer's voice was deep and raspy. His hand moved from my belly up to my tits, and he cupped them again like before. "Feel both of our cocks inside you?"

I nodded, licking my lips. Link moved, pulling his hips back before thrusting into me again.

"Fuck, she's so damn tight," he grunted. He was looking down, watching closely as his shaft disappeared inside of me.

The other three around us watched as well, but I knew they weren't the only ones. The people at this bar weren't focused on their own conversations anymore. What was happening here was way more interesting. Way more entertaining.

I was being shared by five men, fucked by two at the same time while the other three patiently waited their turn.

ARCHER

I felt Link's cock slide in and out of her, pressing against my own internally. I felt Sinclair's body go limp, and I started to worry that she would soon pass out from the intensity she was feeling.

She liked to push her limits, and while I would make sure not to have her miss out on everything that was happening in and around her, I would let her be in charge of what she was able to handle for a while longer.

I wasn't moving too much, occasionally thrusting my hips upward to adjust myself, but other than that, it was Link being the one to fuck Sinclair.

He was already close, groaning, and muttering curses through his gritted teeth.

"Please..." Sin whispered, her voice barely audible.

I squeezed her tits with my left hand and moved my right down to her clit. "Easy," I told her, wanting to keep her with us. "Stay with us."

"I'm trying," she breathed.

I kissed her shoulder and circled her clit with my fingers. That wouldn't help her much. She'd soon have another orgasm, then another, until she felt lightheaded.

I was pushing it now, but I couldn't help it.

"AAAH!"

"That's it, darling. Clench that pussy around my cock. Fuck...that's tight." Link tensed, and shortly after, he was emptying his load inside of her.

She cried out again, and her body started shaking as she reached her own climax.

I tightened my arm around her, holding her in place as she arched her back, only making me bury myself deeper into her.

She quickly realized what she was doing, and I smirked. "There's no escaping, kitten. I'll stay buried deep in this tight asshole while my friends take turns fucking you. Better get used to it."

She couldn't reply, but the way her body reacted to my words said enough.

Chapter 11

SINCLAIR

I was in and out of consciousness.

My mind was mostly awake, acknowledging everything that was happening, but after the second time of them taking turns, I couldn't keep my brain functioning the way I wanted to.

I was certain that my words didn't actually come out of me either. They were echoes in my mind, but they never left my lips.

It was Renner's turn again. He had been the roughest with me tonight, and every time he thrusted into me, he gripped my thighs tightly, leaving marks on my skin.

"She's out of it," he grunted as he continued to fuck me.

He was talking to Archer who was still inside of me, still stretching my ass, and still holding me tightly against his body.

I could hear their voices in the distance although they were all so close.

I should've stopped this before they went for round two, but I was too weak to do so.

"She'll be fine," Tabor said, his voice sounding annoyed.

"Sin," Archer whispered in my ear, nudging my side with his hand.

"Mm-hmm." I managed to open my eyes, but everything around me was a blur. Still, I didn't stop them. "More."

"You sure, kitten?"

I nodded.

"Look at me," he demanded, his hand coming up to cup my throat. He tilted my head to the side, and my eyes met his. "Shit, love, you're pale."

"I'm okay," I promised him. I could go for a while longer, but that was mostly my stubbornness talking. I didn't want to ruin the night for them.

Shit, was I really at the point where men's needs were more important than my own?

Fuck it.

I'd snap out of this soon enough.

I felt another orgasm build inside of me. I lost count of how many I had in the past hour. They might've not all been real orgasms.

My body reacted to the littlest of their moves and touches.

"Finish, then step away. All of you," Archer demanded.

Renner continued to push into me, and soon enough, I felt his cock throbbing inside of me. He was close, and I was finally starting to realize that I needed this to come to an end.

I needed rest. Space. I needed sleep.

"Goddamn. We destroyed this pussy, huh? Can't take any more, can you?" Renner said, his voice threatening.

I looked at him, keeping my eyes open with all the little strength I had left inside of me.

"Yeah, look at those eyes. Nothing left in them," he muttered with a smirk.

He acted as if he had defeated me, and I didn't like that one bit. I was all for having fun and pushing limits, but I didn't like when men used me. And Renner was making me feel that way.

He acted as if he owned me.

Just as he came inside of me, I started pushing against his chest. "Off!" I cried. "Get off me!"

"Damn, you getting feisty now?" He laughed in my face, and I punched his hard chest again.

"Off!"

"Get away from her," Archer demanded, keeping his voice calm.

Renner pulled out of me and stepped back, then Archer gently pushed me off him, making me stand before him.

He got up then, and I turned to him to steady myself.

"Sure you're okay?" he asked, his eyes wandering all over my face. "Think that was too much for you," he added, worriedly.

I didn't respond. I felt dizzy.

"Here, sit," he then told me, helping me sit down on the bench. He quickly grabbed his shirt and put it over my body, then he grabbed his jeans and put them back on. "Watch her while I go grab some water. Make sure she stays awake."

"Don't worry," one of his friends said. I was too far gone to know who it was.

I closed my eyes again, leaning my head back against the wall, and trying to focus on my breathing.

The air in here was thick. Cigarette smoke and the scent of alcohol were all around me, and even if I didn't drink or smoke that night, I felt intoxicated.

I needed Archer to come back, but during my wait, I passed out.

ARCHER

I trusted my friends with my own damn life, and I would do anything to protect them from assholes who wanted to start shit, but when I came back from behind the bar to get water for my girl, I was ready to drop the glass and punch the shit out of one of them.

"GET THE FUCK OFF HER!" I roared, pushing passed Link and Ford.

"I told him not to—"

"OFF!" I grabbed Renner's neck with one hand, pulling him back and away from Sinclair. "I told you not to fucking touch her anymore!"

My girl was lying on the bench, face down, and her body limp. She was unconscious, and when I got to her, I had to make sure she was still breathing.

"I'm sorry, baby," I whispered, brushing back her hair to see her face. "I'll get you out of here," I promised.

"Archer," Link called out to me, and I turned to look at him—unable to hide my anger.

"What!"

"Better go handle Renner. We got her."

I knew I could trust them, but I would've thought the same about Renner just minutes ago.

"Go. Before you regret not getting to beat the shit out of him."

My jaw tightened, and I turned back to Sinclair, making sure she was alright. Well, she wasn't really, but she would be.

"Take her to the back and put blankets around her," I told them. "I'll be right back."

I pressed a kiss to Sin's forehead before getting up and making my way toward the back entrance where I knew Renner ran off to.

He liked to park his car in the back, for whatever damn reason I never understood, but that would come in handy tonight.

He was about to open the backdoor when I gripped his shoulder and pulled him back, making him turn around.

I swung my arm, ready to break his fucking jaw, and as he tried to stop me, my fist met his face forcefully.

I heard something crack, and when he came back up, his bleeding nose confirmed that I had, indeed, broken his nose.

"What the fuck, man?" he groaned, lifting his hand to cover his fracture.

I gripped his collar with both hands and pushed him against the wall, getting closer to his face. "You've broken my damn trust, *my friend*. Don't think you'll get away with this without fucking consequences."

I used my knee to strike him in the stomach, and he bent over again, groaning in pain. It took him a moment to catch his breath, and when I pushed him against the wall again, he was brave enough to speak. "She's a fucking toy. Why the hell are you mad at me for using her?"

That would've been a valid thing to say if I hadn't made it perfectly clear that Sinclair was mine—no matter if I shared her with them.

"You crossed a damn line, man," I told him, using my fist this time to strike him in the face again.

It was his jaw that had to endure pain this time.

"That's enough." Tabor's voice rang through the room. "Let him go. And you, don't show your face here ever again."

I pushed against Renner's chest, then stepped away and watched him stumble to the side. "You can't ban me from this bar."

"I just did," Tabor stated, his voice calm and his face serious. "Get the fuck out of my bar."

Renner watched us both in disbelief, as if he hadn't just assaulted my girl while she was unconscious.

"You heard him. Out."

Renner's glare was vengeful, but I was certain that he would never show his face here or near any of us ever again.

Once he finally came to realize that there was nothing he could say to make this better, he turned and left through the backdoor, leaving a trail of blood on the ground.

"Take me to her," I told Tabor without giving another thought to the man I used to call a friend, and I followed Tabor down the hallway.

Once she'd wake up, she'd remember everything that happened tonight, and I didn't want to lose her.

I had to fix this.

I wouldn't forgive myself for what I let happen to her otherwise.

Chapter 12

SINCLAIR

My head was throbbing, and I couldn't explain why.

I hadn't had alcohol, and I knew I had been eating and drinking enough water to avoid headaches.

So why was there a pounding in my head?

And where the hell was I?

Relief washed over me when I opened my eyes and found myself in Archer's bedroom. He lived in a penthouse, way up high in one of the city's highest buildings.

He had taken me here before, but we rarely made it to the bedroom.

I had taken baths and showers in his bathroom though, so I walked through this room more than I stayed in it.

It was dark out, and it had to be the middle of the night. I closed my eyes again, needing another minute to come to my senses.

There were voices coming from the living room, and I was instantly reminded of what happened last night.

Renner.

His hands on my body.

His groans and threats.

Then there was darkness.

I opened my eyes again, feeling extremely sick to my stomach. I had to get to the bathroom, but the second I sat up, I immediately bent over the side of the bed and heaved.

My body ached and my toes curled, and I clung to the mattress to avoid falling over and right into my vomit.

"Kitten." Archer's voice was full of worry. When he reached me, he pulled back my hair with one hand and rubbed my back with his other. "That'll make you feel better," he assured, his words gentle and empathic.

Once my stomach was emptied, I sat back up and wiped the back of my hand over my lips. My eyes filled with tears from how uncomfortable throwing up made me feel, then I started crying at the reminder of what Renner had done to me last night.

"Is he here?" I asked, scared to see that man again.

Archer's brows furrowed. "That motherfucker won't ever step foot in this apartment again. Tabor, Link, and Ford are here. We took care of him, and he won't come near you again," he assured.

I studied him as he cupped my face with both hands, brushing my cheeks with his thumbs. I waited for him to say more, watching as his face went from serious to guilty.

"I'm sorry. I shouldn't have let that happen. I should've stayed with you. Hell, I shouldn't have taken you to that bar. I broke your trust and I loathe myself for that."

I slowly shook my head, my frown deepening. "Don't...it wasn't your fault."

"I brought you there, and he used you. He fucking used you and I won't forgive myself for that. You're hurting, and it's all my fucking fault."

"No, Archer!" More sobs escaped me as I pushed myself up from under the covers, kneeling next to him while reaching my hands to touch his face. "You did nothing to hurt me. It was him who took advantage." My words didn't sound as strong as I wanted them to, but I needed Archer to know that if anything, he was the one who saved me. "I'm just glad I'm here with you," I finally whispered.

He lowered his head, and I felt his jaw tighten.

I moved my hands to his neck then, resting my forehead against his. "I'll be okay because of you."

A sigh left him. "You're not angry? I dragged you to that bar and let my friends have you. Then he ruined everything. Used you."

I've been fascinated by Archer ever since I met him. I was amazed at how he carried himself. How self-assured he was, but never in an arrogant way. But I was starting to like this side of him.

I smiled and shook my head. "Up until what happened with Renner, everything was perfect."

Talking about it helped a lot. Should've talked about it the first time it happened, but at fourteen, you don't talk about the trauma you went through. You keep it inside of you, tell yourself to be strong, and try to forget it because life has to go on.

I was older now. Old enough to not let a man like Renner ruin me a second time.

I would heal from this. Not only because of Archer, but also because of myself. I was older, mentally stronger. And if I'd see that asshole again, and would happen to have a gun with me, I will shoot him.

Right in the nuts.

ARCHER

Sinclair was stronger than I ever could've imagined.

I knew what Renner did to her would still linger on her mind, but I would give her all the time and support she needed.

When I first met Sinclair, I hadn't planned on sticking around for long. I imagined her being yet another hookup. A fun time I would keep to myself and never share with my friends.

But everything turned out differently.

I didn't regret bringing her to Tabor's bar, and I also didn't regret sharing Sin with them.

And even if I couldn't have known Renner would turn on me, I did regret my friendship with him.

Some people were unpredictable in their actions, and Renner had proven that even the most loyal ones in your life had the audacity to turn on you.

Ford and Link had taken care of him. Made sure that from now on, he was a ghost in this town. All connections we had to him were cut. He was damn lucky I didn't break his damn neck last night.

I held Sinclair in my arms, comforting her as best as I could. I still felt as if I had failed her, but the way she caressed my neck told me that she truly wasn't upset with me.

"It's still early," I whispered into her hair. "But I need to clean this. You can't sleep in here like this."

"I'm sorry," she said quietly.

"Don't." My body tensed, and I gripped her hair at the back of her head tightly. "Don't ever apologize. Let me get you something clean to wear. We'll sleep in the guestroom."

She didn't argue and let me hold her a while longer.

Chapter 13

ARCHER

"How are you feeling?" Tabor asked Sin as we walked into the living room.

She was firmly holding on to my hand with both of hers. She wasn't hiding, but she was standing so close to me that only her head peeked around me.

"I'm okay," she told him, her eyes big as she took in the scene. It was almost four in the morning, and the guys had come to my place after making sure Renner was far enough away.

"Come sit with us," Link then said, patting the spot on the couch next to him. "There are some things Archer has to talk to you about."

Sinclair looked up at me with question in her eyes. I let go of her hand and rubbed her back before nodding toward the couch. "You should be getting some rest, but

I don't think I can get any myself if I'm not opening up to you about some things."

She looked confused. Granted, I would be too if someone would act so damn mysterious.

Sinclair hesitated, and though she trusted me, there was fear in her eyes. "Am I safe? I mean...am I safe *here*?"

"Yes." I hated that she felt so unsure that she asked a question like that. "You're safe here. I have some things I haven't told you, and I want you to know everything about me—about us." I had to regain her trust. Fully.

She shifted her gaze to the guys, and after taking a moment to reflect on the situation, she finally walked over to sit next to Link.

He respectfully moved further away to give her more space, and I took a seat on her other side, resting my hand on her thigh.

"I'll get her some water," Ford said, and Sinclair watched him get up and head over to the open kitchen.

Then her eyes met mine, and I gave her a gentle smile, hoping I wasn't making her nervous or scared.

I waited for Ford to be back, handing Sin the water. She thanked him quietly and took a sip, and I watched her, wondering how a woman like her must be feeling in a room full of men.

Men who hours before were inside of her, pleasuring themselves and her.

"I'm ready," she told me. She kept the glass in her hands, and I figured she needed to hold on to something other than the man who would shortly reveal a couple of things about himself.

I cleared my throat and moved my gaze to each of my friends, then my eyes were on her again. "The guys and I have known each other since college. We've spent all our lives together, been through a lot of shit, conquered the worst situations with each other. But most of all, we've always supported one another. We built our businesses around each other's. Made sure that everything we do goes smoothly. We grew together, made incredible deals with other businesses. But we also made enemies." I looked at the guys again, rubbing my hands together as I thought of the right words to use for this next part. "You may remember us talking about a guy named Manny."

Sinclair's brows furrowed, then she nodded. "I remember."

"Manny has messed with us once before but we gave him a second chance because Renner assured us that it won't happen again. He owns a company that develops software to protect businesses from hackers. Turns out he used his powers to get into our secret systems and bank accounts. Long story short...he was about to fuck us over once again. Last night, Ford and Link tracked Renner down and they found him in his office downtown, making a damn phone call to Manny. They were planning something, but we stopped them."

Sinclair was watching me intensely, listening carefully to every word I said. When her frown deepened, I knew she'd have more questions about this. "I thought Renner is your friend."

"He *was*," Ford stated, and Tabor murmured a curse before adding more.

"He betrayed us. And he hurt you. We'll make sure that motherfucker won't show his face around us ever again."

Sinclair let our words sink in, then she took another sip. She set the glass down on the coffee table this time, then she looked at me with gentle eyes. "What kind of business do you have?"

She wasn't interested in hearing more of Renner, and we all took the hint.

"I own two real estate companies. I manage, sell, buy, and invest in properties and land. Mostly to people who have lots of money. Link and Ford own the best law firm in the country, and Tabor is in the alcohol industry," I said with an amused grin on my face.

"You won't ever call it by its name, will you?" Tabor shook his head and chuckled, then he looked at Sinclair. "I own a liquor company and multiple bars and clubs in the state."

All that information was a lot to take in for Sinclair, but she took her time to let it all sink in. Her eyes moved to Tabor, then Link, Ford, and then they finally met mine again. "So...you're basically all millionaire best friends."

It was a statement that never fazed me, even after years of earning good money.

We chuckled, and I reached for her hand. "We're best friends. Our money doesn't have to do with anything. We worked hard and got our reward."

"Apparently, some don't deserve to be rewarded, no matter how fucking hard they work," Tabor spat.

"We won't discuss him any longer," I told him, giving him a warning glance.

"What else is there? Any more I should know about you?" Sinclair asked, grasping my attention again.

I looked at her and thought of one thing that might be important for her to know. "There are some dangerous situations at times. None we're personally involved in, but we've had groups of criminals attack our businesses before. We got that all under control though. Nothing you have to worry about, alright? We got the law on our side."

She studied me for a while, then moved her eyes back to the others, watching them just as intensely while she decided on how to feel about all of this.

Her fingers tightened around mine, then she finally spoke. "Okay. I trust you guys."

In that moment, I promised myself to keep her safe no matter what.

Little did I know that the ones who betrayed me would do it all over again.

Epilogue
SINCLAIR

Two months later

Trauma had a funny way of living inside someone.

For some it was hard to shake it off, to keep on living without constantly thinking about all the pain.

For others, life went on. Trauma was just a bump in the road for them.

I was somewhat in the middle of it. I didn't forget about all the pain but I also managed to ignore the memories.

Personally, I was certain that the way you handled trauma had to do with the people you surrounded yourself with.

Before Archer, I thought about that one night when I was fourteen almost every day. But the longer he was in my life, the less I thought of it.

And now, it wasn't only Archer who took my mind off the negative things in life.

Tabor, Link, and Ford were just as good at making me forget.

I couldn't quite explain what kind of relationship we were in, but with my heart growing heavier every time I spent time with them, and the guys being particularly sweet and protective, I knew there had to be something bigger than I ever would've expected.

Of course, my feelings for Archer had always been different. I had fallen in love with him the same night that the incident with Renner occurred.

I called the other three men *bonuses*.

They all had different characteristics, were all very busy with work, and it would take me a while to get used to them being around as often as Archer was. Still, I wouldn't push them away.

They had explained to me that none of them were ready to commit to a relationship, but if I let them, I only belonged to them and vice versa.

I was okay with that. I liked being shared, but I sure as hell didn't like to share.

I spent lots of time at Archer's office, watching him work, take calls, write emails. But he also watched me while I sat there on the lounger in the corner of his office, often times teasing him by spreading my legs and lifting my skirts.

The others often came by to have lunch with us, and almost every time, we ended up fucking in Archer's office afterward.

Today was one of those times.

It was a stormy, rainy day, and the view from the very top of Archer's building wasn't as pretty as usual.

But the view wasn't as important. I had other things to see.

I was on all fours in the middle of the office, with Archer kneeling behind me, teasing me with his tip at my entrance.

The other three were standing in front of me, all stroking their cocks while watching me closely.

Ford and Tabor had already come inside of me, and Link had—surprisingly—politely asked to come in my mouth.

I said yes and was now patiently waiting for him to come closer and let me suck his dick.

He got down on one knee, reaching out his left hand to cup the back of my head, then he inched closer until his tip touched my lips. "Open up, darling."

I looked up at him through my lashes as pulled him inside my mouth. His hardness slid along my tongue until his tip hit the back of my throat, and he pulled back to give me a moment to breathe again.

I didn't need to though. I wanted him to be rough, and so I leaned in again, pulling him back inside my mouth until I gagged.

"Beautiful. Fucking beautiful," he muttered. He put both hands on either side of my head, holding me still as he started thrusting his hips.

A sharp pain rushed through me as Archer slapped my ass, and after hearing him cuss under his breath, he pulled out of me and said, "Gonna fill this asshole with my piss before coming inside that tight pussy."

I wanted to beg for it, but I couldn't speak with Link's cock in my mouth. Instead, I arched my back and pushed against him, needy for more.

"You want that, don't you? My dirty little kitten. Fuck. So damn sinful."

He pushed his cock back into my asshole, and while Link continued to face fuck me, I waited impatiently for Archer to fill me with his urine.

A moan escaped me when I felt the warmth inside of me and dripping down my inner thighs, and Archer groaned, emptying himself.

"So fucking hot," I heard Tabor mutter, and I had to silently agree.

I loved how dirty they were, and how open I was to these things. There definitely weren't many people who would let this happen to them, but I didn't care for others.

I had my men, and they could do whatever they wanted to me.

"ARGH!" Link fisted my hair tightly as his body tensed, and as I looked up again, I knew he was close.

He wanted to hold back but I couldn't wait to finally taste him.

My lips tightened around his shaft, and I sucked harder, making him pulsate uncontrollably.

His knee was shaking, and as his tip hit the back of my throat one last time, he pulled back and cupped my jaw to keep my mouth open.

"Goddamn!" he grunted as he unloaded on my tongue, his eyes never leaving me. "That's it. Fuck, yes! Swallow. Come on, baby, swallow all my cum."

I swallowed all of it, with maybe one or two drops dripping down my chin. Link brushed those away with his thumb before pushing it back into my mouth. "I said all of it. Don't want any to go to waste."

I sucked his thumb, then I watched him get up and stand next to Tabor.

I was certain that the three of them were about to make themselves come once more, and I would be right here waiting for them to cover me in their semen.

Archer's hands gripped my ass tightly, and as he pulled out of me, his piss leaked out of me, wetting the laminate floor beneath me.

Without a warning, I felt his mouth on my pussy, his tongue licking from my clit all the way up to my asshole. He was tasting himself, and he knew I loved when he did that.

I moaned and leaned forward, sticking my ass up into the air and resting my head on my forearms.

He played with my pussy, teasing my clit, then he pushed his tongue inside of me before pulling back and using his cock again.

He started fucking me hard, and my pussy soon started pulsating and clenching around his length.

"Take it like a good girl. Fuck, I love this pussy," he growled, and his words warmed me from the inside. It was already a big deal for him to use the word love, but what he said next sent me spiraling, reaching the greatest climax I ever had. "I love you, Sinclair."

I fully realized what he had announced in front of his friends just then when I calmed down.

I slowly opened my eyes as his cum filled me, and I turned my head to look at him with the faintest smile. "I love you too, Archer."

Despite us having a sweet moment, the other three decided that they wanted to be part of this too.

They shot their loads on my back, some of their cum landing on my hair which didn't bother me.

Their loud groans filled the room, and once they were finished, Archer pulled me up and turned me around to face him.

There was a smug grin on his lips. He cupped my face and kissed me. "Should've kept that in for when we're alone," he whispered against my lips.

I laughed softly. I was holding on to his shoulders, unable to kneel there without any support. "It's okay," I told him, looking into his eyes. "I know you meant it. And so did I."

"Good. Because I'm not taking it back." He kissed me again, pulling me tighter against him, making me deepen the kiss.

"Don't wanna interrupt this moment, but we gotta clean her up. We gotta get back to work," Ford said.

I pulled back and looked at them, then I tried to see what my back looked like now that I was covered in cum. "I think I need a shower."

"Yeah, you do. I'll take you downstairs to the gym where you can take a shower," Archer said.

We both got up, and Tabor wrapped a suit jacket around me. "Keep this on to get to the gym."

"Don't you need your jacket?" I asked, looking at him.

"I got another one back at the office. Don't you worry."

I smiled and gave him a quick nod. "Thank you, Tabor."

I watched as the guys all got dressed, and once they were ready, I looked at them with admiration.

My cheeks flushed when I noticed them waiting for me to speak but no words came out of me.

Therefore, I stepped closer and hoped for them to understand what I was going for.

To my luck, they all opened their arms and pulled me into a big, warm group hug.

I leaned into them and closed my eyes, smiling at their embrace.

They chuckled, and Archer was the one to speak first. "We got you, kitten. We'll take good care of you."

"In any possible way," Tabor added, making me laugh.

"Thank you. I couldn't be happier."

My heart was incredibly full, and they would make sure it would stay that way forever.

...At least they tried.

Find More Seven Rue

Website: www.authorsevenrue.com
Amazon: Seven Rue
Instagram: @sevenrue
TikTok: @authorsevenrue
Reader Group on Facebook: Seven Rue's Taboos

Made in the USA
Las Vegas, NV
04 October 2024

96316672R00066